Four Little Kittens

BY KATHLEEN N. DALY

PICTURES BY
ADRIANA MAZZA SAVIOZZI

A GOLDEN BOOK • NEW YORK
Western Publishing Company, Inc.
Racine, Wisconsin 53404

Once upon a time, four kittens were born in a corner of a barn.

"I wonder what kind of cats they'll grow up to be," thought the mother cat.

She licked her four new babies proudly. They were still tiny. Their eyes were sealed shut, and they could only mew, and snuggle close to their mother's warm side.

In a few days, the kittens opened their eyes. Each day they grew a little bigger, and a little stronger. "And a great deal naughtier," thought Mother Cat, as they pounced on her twitchy tail.

"Children," she said one day, "the time has come
for you to decide what kind of cats you will be."

"Tell us, tell us," mewed the kittens, "what kind
of cats there are."

Mother Cat sat up straight, and half closed her
green eyes, and began.

"There are Alley Cats.

"An Alley Cat is long and lean. He slinks like a shadow, sleeps where he can, eats what he finds.

"A free cat is he—no manners to mind, no washing of paws, no sheathing of claws. He does what he likes, and nobody knows but he.

"Your Uncle Tom is an Alley Cat. Many friends he has, and they make fine music at night, to the moon.

"His enemies are stray dogs, and turning wheels, and cold, sleety rain. He's a wild and clever cat, the Alley Cat."

"That is the life for me," said Tuff, the biggest kitten. And off he went, to be an Alley Cat, like bold Uncle Tom.

"Now Uncle Tar was a Ship's Cat," Mother Cat went on. "A splendid cat he was, with a ship for a home, and sailors for friends.

"A Ship's Cat visits seaports a thousand miles away, and talks to foreign cats, and chases foreign rats that try to come aboard.

"A brave cat he is, a jolly, roving cat, a Ship's Cat. And many are the tales your Uncle Tar could tell."

"That is the life for me," said Luff, the second kitten. And off he went, to be a Ship's Cat, like jolly Uncle Tar.

"And of course," said Mother Cat, "there are Farm Cats.

"I am a Farm Cat, a useful cat. I catch the mice and chase the rats, while the farmer sleeps at night.

"I live in the barn on a bed of straw—no House Cat am I.

"A Farm Cat can talk to all the animals that live
on the farm.

"A splendid, useful, strong cat is the Farm Cat—
though I say it myself."

"That is the life for me," said Ruff, the third kitten. And off he went, to be a Farm Cat, like his
mother. Mother Cat purred.

Now the smallest, youngest kitten was called Muff. Muff was gentle, and playful, and pretty, and always kept her white paws clean.

Muff's mother sighed and said, "Muff, I don't think you are an Alley Cat. I don't think you are a Ship's Cat, or even a Farm Cat. I don't know what kind of cat you are."

And off went Mother Cat, to catch a nice, fat mouse for dinner.

Sadly, Muff wandered out of the barn.

She caught sight of Ruff, getting ready to spring on a great big rat. Muff shivered, and crept by as quietly as she could.

"I couldn't be a Farm Cat," said Muff, "because I'm *afraid* of big rats."

Muff wandered out of the farm and down to the village.

She saw plump little Tuff, doing his best to look lean and wild like an Alley Cat.

"Wuff, wuff," barked a little stray dog, and Tuff arched his back, and bristled his fur, and spat and hissed in his best Alley Cat way.

The little dog ran away. And so did Muff.

Down to the river she ran, and she saw Luff on a
big ship in the harbor.

The sailors were busy with ropes and things, but
already Luff had curled up in a place where he
wouldn't be in the way. Soon Luff would be visit-
ing cats a thousand miles away, just like Uncle Tar.

Muff waved good-by. "I wish I knew what kind
of cat I am," she sighed. Then she had to run out of
the way as a bicycle came by.

It began to rain, and Muff got cold and wet. She didn't like that at all, and she shook her wet paws crossly.

She lay down to sleep on a lumpy pile of sacks. She didn't like that very much, either.

She was cold and hungry and cross, and when a

big hand picked her up, she spat and hissed for all the world like an Alley Cat.

But the big hand put her into a big, warm pocket, and after a few more angry squawks, and a sad little mew, Muff fell asleep.

When next she opened her eyes, Muff was in a house.

There were cushions and carpets and curtains. There was a warm, crackling fire.

There was a little girl with soft, gentle hands.

"Oh, what a lovely kitten," said the little girl. "Oh, I wanted a kitten so much. Now I won't be lonely any more."

The little girl gave Muff a saucer of cream.

Muff drank it all, with one white foot in the saucer to keep it steady. Then she washed her paw, and licked her whiskers.

This was *much* better than fat mice for dinner.

The little girl played with Muff. She dangled a
string, and Muff jumped and pounced in her
prettiest way, and the little girl laughed with delight.
Muff purred.

This was much better than running away from
barking dogs, and turning wheels.

The little girl lifted Muff onto her warm lap, and stroked Muff's fur.

"Oh, it's nice to have a kitten," said the little girl happily.

Muff purred loudly.

This was much better than a pile of lumpy sacks, or even a bed of straw.

"This is the life for me," purred Muff. "I know what kind of cat I am, at last.

"I'm a cushion and cream cat, a purring cat, a cuddlesome cat, a playful cat, a little girl's cat—I'm a House Cat!"

And so all four kittens lived happily ever after—
Tuff in his alley, because he was an Alley Cat,
Ruff on his farm, because he was a Farm Cat,
Luff on his ship, because he was a Ship's Cat, and
Muff on her cushions, in her house, with her
little girl, because she was a House Cat.